Rylant
nt, Cynthia
vnie & Pearl step out /
99

BROWNIE & PEARL
Step Out

by CYNTHIA RYLANT
pictures by BRIAN BIGGS

Ready-to-Read

Simon Spotlight
New York London Toronto Sydney New Delhi

Look who is stepping out.
It is Brownie and Pearl!

They are going to a party.

It is a birthday party.

Cats are invited.

There is the house.
See all the balloons?

Now it is time to knock.

Uh-oh.

Brownie feels shy.

Maybe she will go home.

But Pearl is not shy.

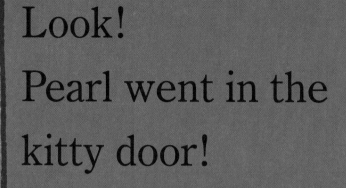

Look!
Pearl went in the
kitty door!

Now Brownie
has to knock.

Welcome to the party, Brownie!

Brownie likes the party.
She plays games.

She eats cake.

She eats ice cream.

She eats more ice cream.

Brownie is happy that
Pearl went in the kitty door.

Pearl is happy too!

For Pascale
—C. R.

For Sacha, Harry, and Jake
—B. B.

SIMON SPOTLIGHT
An imprint of Simon & Schuster Children's Publishing Division
1230 Avenue of the Americas, New York, New York 10020
Text copyright © 2010 by Cynthia Rylant
Illustrations copyright © 2010 by Brian Biggs
SIMON SPOTLIGHT, READY-TO-READ, and colophon are registered
trademarks of Simon & Schuster, Inc.
For information about special discounts for bulk purchases, please contact
Simon & Schuster Special Sales at 1-866-506-1949 or business@simonandschuster.com.
The Simon & Schuster Speakers Bureau can bring authors to your live event.
For more information or to book an event contact the Simon & Schuster Speakers
Bureau at 1-866-248-3049 or visit our website at www.simonspeakers.com.
Manufactured in the United States of America 0314 LAK
First Edition
2 4 6 8 10 9 7 5 3 1
Library of Congress Cataloging-in-Publication Data
Rylant, Cynthia.
Brownie & Pearl step out / by Cynthia Rylant ; illustrated by Brian Biggs. — First edition.
pages cm. — (Ready-to-read)
Summary: A little girl named Brownie arrives at a birthday party feeling shy while her cat Pearl
confidently enters through the "kitty door."
[1. Parties—Fiction. 2. Cats—Fiction.] I. Biggs, Brian illustrator. II. Title.
III. Title: Brownie and Pearl step out.
PZ7.R982Bt 2014
[E]—dc23
2013024921
ISBN 978-1-4814-0313-9 (pbk)
ISBN 978-1-4814-0314-6 (hc)
ISBN 978-1-4424-3909-2 (eBook)